D1123764

A Rookie reader®

Balls

Written by
Melanie Davis Jones

Illustrated by Linda Bronson

Children's Press®
A Division of Scholastic Inc.
New York • Toronto • London • Auckland • Sydney
Mexico City • New Delhi • Hong Kong
Danbury, Connecticut

Dear Parents/Educators,

Welcome to Rookie Ready to Learn. Each Rookie Reader in this series includes additional age-appropriate Let's Learn Together activity pages that help your young child to be better prepared when starting school. *Balls* offers opportunities for you and your child to talk about the important social/emotional skill of **relating to others**.

Here are early-learning skills you and your child will encounter in the *Balls* Let's Learn Together pages:

• Rhyming

• Math: even numbers

• Narrative skill: describing

We hope you enjoy sharing this delightful, enhanced reading experience with your early learner.

Library of Congress Cataloging-in-Publication Data

Jones, Melanie Davis.
  Balls / written by Melanie Davis Jones ; illustrated by Linda Bronson.
    p. cm. -- (Rookie ready to learn)
  Summary: Rhyming text introduces the many types of balls and how they are used.
Includes suggested learning activities.

  ISBN 978-0-531-26445-4 - ISBN 978-0-531-2674-5 (pbk.)
  [1. Stories in rhyme. 2. Balls (Sporting goods)--Fiction.] I. Bronson, Linda, ill. II. Title. III. Series.
  PZ8.3.J7535Bal 2011
  [E]--dc21
                          2010049905

CHILDREN'S PRESS, and ROOKIE READY TO LEARN, and associated logos are trademarks and or registered trademarks of Scholastic Library Publishing. SCHOLASTIC and associated logos are trademarks or registered trademarks of Scholastic, Inc.

1 2 3 4 5 6 7 8 9 10 R 18 17 16 15 14 13 12 11

Balls roll.

Balls spin.

Balls knock down bowling pins.

Balls zoom.
Balls fly.

Balls pop up to the sky.

**Balls bounce.
Balls soar.**

13

Balls go in the net to score.

**Balls go up.
Balls come down.**

Count how many balls are round.

**Balls are big.
Balls are small.**

Count how many balls in all.

Congratulations!

You just finished reading *Balls* and learned about all the fun you can have playing with many different kinds of balls.

About the Author
Melanie Davis Jones works as a reading specialist in Warner Robins, Georgia. Mrs. Jones has a husband, Randy, and three sons, who are all crazy for sports.

About the Illustrator
Linda Bronson is the illustrator of several acclaimed children's books, including *Teatime with Emma Buttersnap* and *The Circus Alphabet*.

Balls

Let's learn together!

Take Me Out to the Ball Game

(Sing this song to the tune of
"Take Me Out to the Ball Game.")

Take me out
to the ball game.
Take me out
with the crowd.
Buy me some peanuts
and Cracker Jack.
I don't care if I
never get back.
Oh it's root, root, root
for the home team.
If they don't win,
it's a shame.
For it's one, two, three
strikes, you're out,
At the old ball game.

PARENT TIP: This is a great opportunity to talk about the fun of watching other people play games. When your child watches a baseball game or other team sport, take that opportunity to emphasize that teams work together and that no matter who wins, it's the fun of the game that counts.

Picture Rhyme

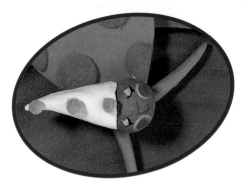

You saw a clown hat and a baseball hat in the story. Look at the pictures below and name each picture.

Point to the pictures that rhyme with *hat*.

ball

cat

bat

bowling pin

PARENT TIP: Rhyming games build an awareness of sounds, which is an important early reading concept. Your child will begin to learn that words are made up of sounds that can be separated — and that playing with words can be lots of fun!

My Favorite

Fill in the blanks out loud to tell a story about your favorite sport or game, and whom you like to play it with.

My favorite sport or game is _____.

name of favorite game or sport

I like to play it with _____.

name of friend or family member

One thing I really like about this sport or game is

_____.

description of what you like

Even Number Hunt

Count the balls in each group. Then point to the number that matches.

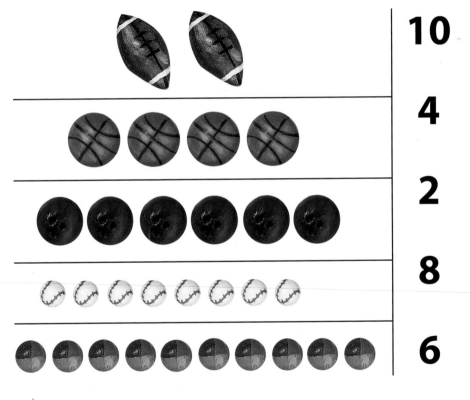

PARENT TIP: Matching quantities to numerals is an early math concept, as is recognizing numerals themselves. Help build numeral recognition anytime by looking for numerals all around you, such as on signs in store windows, on mailboxes, on buildings, or on license plates.

Name That Ball!

There are many different kinds of balls. Follow the path of balls to the toy box. Can you name each ball? Look at the words in the box to help you.

baseball   **basketball**   **football**

START

FINISH

PARENT TIP: Help your child expand her vocabulary by talking about how the different balls are named. For instance, a basketball is called a basketball because it's thrown into a basket, a beach ball is good to play with at the beach, and so on. Balls can be hard or soft, hollow or solid, heavy or light, bouncy or not bouncy!

Ball Toss

In the book, you saw how many different things you can do with a ball. Experiment with a ball you make yourself.

YOU WILL NEED: Aluminum foil

1
Tear off a large sheet of aluminum foil and roll it into a ball.

2
Try to do different things with the foil ball. Try to throw it far, bounce it, spin it, throw it high up into the air and catch it. Which things work? Which things don't work?

3
Try again using a different ball.

Balls Word List (29 Words)

all	down	pins	spin
are	fly	pop	the
balls	go	roll	to
big	how	round	up
bounce	in	score	zoom
bowling	knock	sky	
come	many	small	
count	net	soar	

PARENT TIP: Read this list of all the words in the book. The words *bounce*, *spin*, *zoom*, *roll*, and *fly* are all things that balls do — and are fun for kids to pantomime. List these words in different colors on a separate sheet of paper, and invite your child to act them out.